HUMPHREY
The Wayward Whale

*by Ernest Callenbach and
Christine Leefeldt*

Illustrations by Carl Dennis Buell

HEYDAY BOOKS
Berkeley, California

Humphrey the Humpback Whale lived in the vast Pacific Ocean. From the icy Alaskan waters where he had been feeding all summer to the warm waters where he was now heading, the ocean was home to Humphrey and his friends.

As Humphrey swam south, he and his friends sang songs to each other, mysterious songs that could be heard many miles away. So Humphrey always knew where the other whales in his pod were, day or night. Humphrey and his friends whistled and grunted and squealed, they groaned and mooed and tooted. They beeped and creaked and clicked. They wailed their wild sounds all through the great Pacific deeps.

Text © 1986 by Ernest Callenbach and Christine Leefeldt
Drawings © 1986 by Carl Dennis Buell
Design by Nancy Austin

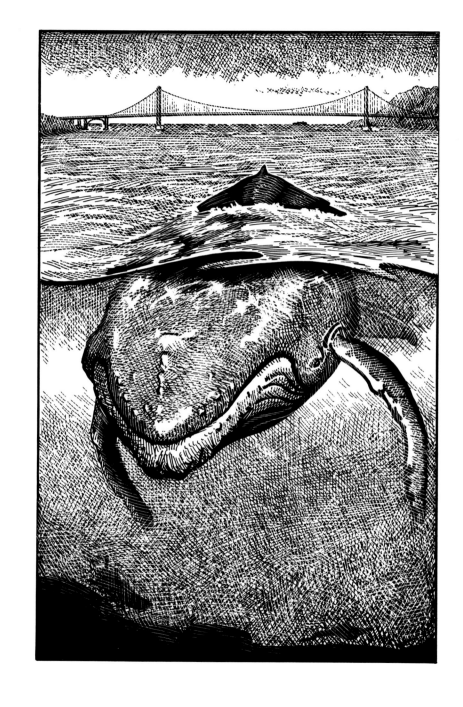

Humphrey was a young whale, not yet fully grown. But he was already forty feet long—as big as a bus. He was huge! Yet his favorite foods were tiny shrimp-like creatures and little fish, which he strained out of the water with the long combs of whalebone in his mouth. Humphrey had been feeding all summer long, and by now he had stored up so much fat that he could live for weeks without eating.

With his powerful tail flukes, Humphrey swam fast and far. He and his pod had already traveled thousands of miles. By the middle of October, he had reached Point Reyes, where eager whale watchers with binoculars gathered to observe migrating whales. Humphrey was about to cross the mouth of San Francisco Bay when he did something very unusual for a whale.

Humphrey left his pod and swam, all by himself, underneath the Golden Gate Bridge and into the Bay!

How different the bay was from Humphrey's ocean home! The water was calmer here, and in some places so shallow that Humphrey's belly nearly rubbed against the bottom. He met creatures he had never known before—sand-sharks and rays gliding along, flounders and clams half-buried in the mud, crabs scuttling on their spindly legs. The water tasted different here. And what confusing sounds Humphrey heard—the sputtering of outboard motors, the clanking of busy freighters.

As night fell, Humphrey came to Alcatraz Island. He raised his giant head out of the water to look around. The bright beam of the lighthouse flashed at him. And the city lights of San Francisco gleamed like a million golden stars.

Humphrey could no longer hear the songs from his pod. Now he was on his own.

At daybreak, a little girl and her father were fishing from a pier on the bay. "Look, Daddy, a whale!" she shouted.

"Don't be silly," said her father. "There aren't any whales in the bay."

"No, Daddy, look!" Just then Humphrey's enormous bumpy head and shiny black back heaved above the water.

"Incredible!" her father yelled. "Hey, everybody," he shouted at the other people fishing from the pier. "There's a whale in the bay!"

Soon Humphrey began following a deepwater ship channel north into San Pablo Bay. He passed an immense whale-like shape—many times larger than any whale he had ever seen. It was a submarine, heading to sea. Humphrey sang a song to it, but the submarine did not answer.

Humphrey turned inland now, where the channel led under the Carquinez Bridge. He passed the town of Crockett, and then Benicia, where another bridge made a high, graceful curve against the sky.

Where in the world was Humphrey going?

Humphrey passed Pittsburg, where the Sacramento River meets Suisun Bay. Word of his visit had now spread far and wide. Hundreds of curious adults and children began to gather along the shores to watch Humphrey. Teachers brought whole classes. Television camera crews took pictures of Humphrey for the evening news. People lined up patiently, hoping to see the tall spout of spray that Humphrey sometimes made when he breathed, or to get a glimpse of his graceful tail.

"Thar he blows!" people yelled, because that is what they thought they should yell when they saw a whale.

People were delighted at Humphrey's visit, but they wondered what he was doing. Had he come into the bay to escape some danger? Was he too young to know where he was going? Had he lost his sense of direction because he was sick? Was he looking for food? Was he curious to see new waters and have new adventures? Would he turn around soon and head back to his ocean home?

Nobody knew. There wasn't a clue.

Humphrey pushed on upstream, deeper into the delta, where fresh river water flows in many narrow channels called sloughs. Humphrey's flippers, fifteen feet long, often brushed the bottom. He twisted and turned through the maze of channels. His tail stirred up the mud where catfish and crayfish and turtles hid. Humphrey saw a muskrat swimming past, returning to the underwater entrance of its nest. He saw a heron, standing in the water on long legs, hoping to catch frogs. He passed flocks of ducks and geese. They too had migrated from the chilly north. He swam under the drawbridge at Rio Vista. And finally, almost seventy miles from the wild ocean that was his natural home, Humphrey squeezed between a row of poles that held up an old bridge, and came into Cache Slough.

Here Humphrey stayed. Scientists who had come to study Humphrey kept watch over him day and night. As the days passed and Humphrey did not budge, they became worried. Would the fresh water hurt his skin or his eyes or his insides? Would he crack his bones by banging against the bottom? Would he get stuck in a shallow spot and not be able to swim away? Would he ever return to the sea?

Nobody knew. There wasn't a clue.

Scientists and government workers held a meeting. "Let's help Humphrey," they said.

They collected a fleet of boats. The crew members on each boat lowered long pipes part way into the water and banged on them. What a loud, horrid noise they made! They hoped this racket would annoy Humphrey and drive him downstream, back through the poles of the bridge. Humphrey did move toward the bridge, but then circled around and dived under the boats, coming up behind them, as if he were playing hide-and-seek.

"Maybe Humphrey is afraid to go between the poles," someone suggested. Engineers arrived and used heavy machines to clear away the mud, logs and rocks that had gotten caught between the poles of the bridge. Now there was a bigger opening for Humphrey. Would this work? Crew members on

the boats again banged on the pipes and made their horrid noises. Finally, Humphrey swam underneath the Cache Slough Bridge, and the people on the banks and in the boats whooped and cheered with happiness.

But when Humphrey came to the dark bar of shadow made by the Rio Vista Bridge, he refused to go further. "Could the traffic noise from the bridge be bothering Humphrey?" people wondered. They stopped traffic and raised the drawbridge, and again they banged on their pipes. Humphrey went under the bridge.

"Hooray for Humphrey!" everyone shouted.

Would he now swim downriver and home on his own?

Nobody knew. There wasn't a clue.

Once again, Humphrey wouldn't move. Everyone became worried. Some were even afraid that Humphrey might die, away from all his whale friends. What could they do? "Let's play sound recordings of humpbacks gathering to feed," one person suggested. "Maybe Humphrey has grown hungry, and he'll follow these sounds in hopes of finding a meal." Would he? Nobody knew.

From a boat, the scientists played their recordings underwater. Humphrey heard the whale assembly call—long, urgent shrieks. But there weren't any whales. Humphrey slapped the surface loudly with his tail, as whales do when they are angry.

But then, slowly but surely, Humphrey began to follow the boat. He followed it along the marshes of Suisun Bay and under the span of the Benicia Bridge. He followed it under the Carquinez Bridge and across the windy sweep of San Pablo Bay. He followed it under the Richmond Bridge, all the way to Angel Island. He covered fifty miles in a single day!

Humphrey was nearing his ocean home at last. "Keep going, Humphrey!" joyful people yelled from their sailboats as Humphrey passed. And they thought Humphrey was happy too, because he leaped out of the water and came down with an enormous splash.

But oh, no! Just as Humphrey was about to leave the bay for the open ocean, he turned back. "Call all the boats!" someone said.

Boats came from everywhere. There were navy boats, coast guard boats, game warden boats, county sheriff boats, fishing boats, pleasure boats —boats large and small, fast and slow.

While the boats blocked the way so Humphrey could not swim upstream, the recorded feeding sounds called him toward the ocean. For a while he ignored them, but the yups and chirps and cricks and squeaks grew louder. Humphrey stirred. Then slowly he began to follow them toward the Golden Gate Bridge.

When drivers crossing the bridge saw Humphrey and the fleet of boats with him, they stopped their cars right in the middle of the bridge and got out to look. They didn't care about blocking traffic— everyone wanted to see Humphrey! They leaned over the railings and urged Humphrey on.

"Go, Humphrey, go!" they shouted. And when he finally swam under the bridge giving a toot and spouting a great spray of water, they cheered and cheered. "Goodbye, Humphrey!" they called. "We love you!"

Humphrey left the boats behind and headed steadily into the Pacific. People stood on the bridge and all along the ocean shore, watching and watching. Many of them were crying.

Soon Humphrey began to hear, faint and far away, the familiar songs of migrating humpbacks. Singing a song in response, Humphrey flipped his mighty tail, dived deep into the cold, salty sea, and disappeared.

Humphrey had gone home at last.

End Note

Humphrey, a real humpback whale, entered San Francisco Bay on October 10, 1985. and swam out again on November 4. His visit created a stir among scientists as well as among the general public.

Little is known with certainty about the lives of humpback whales. They spend most of their year in relatively shallow ocean areas. Females usually give birth every two years; a newborn humpback is about fourteen to fifteen feet long and weighs about 3,000 pounds. As a baby whale nurses, its mother squirts extremely rich milk into its mouth, so it gains many pounds each day. When fully grown, a humpback may be sixty-two feet long and weigh more than 100,000 pounds.

Humpbacks are the most acrobatic of all whales. They have extremely long flippers, about one third their body length, which they often wave in the air or slap against the sea surface. These huge animals can leap entirely out of the water, and they can stay under water for up to fifteen minutes.

Humpbacks are officially classified as an endangered species. It is estimated that there are only about 2,000 of them in the North Pacific population to which Humphrey belonged, and only about 10,000 worldwide.

Scientists welcomed Humphrey's arrival in San Francisco Bay as an opportunity to study a humpback at close quarters. His motions and habits were carefully monitored. Fresh water did damage his skin, but in several later years he was seen alive and well outside the Golden Gate, swimming with other whales. Some scientists suspect that humpbacks use echolocation as toothed whales do—to "see" underwater by sending out pulses of sound which reflect back from objects. It is possible that such an ability helped Humphrey maneuver through the murky waters of the Delta, although sound recordings made during Humphrey's visit did not prove this.

Many new observations made during Humphrey's stay are now being analyzed and debated. But as to the question of why Humphrey came inland, or why he remained so long, the scientists were in the same fix as the rest of us: nobody knew!

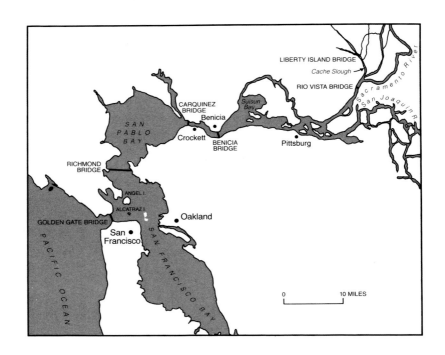

LIBERTY ISLAND BRIDGE

Cache Slough

RIO VISTA BRIDGE

Sacramento River

San Joaquin R.

CARQUINEZ BRIDGE

Suisun Bay

Benicia

*S A N
P A B L O
B A Y*

Crockett

BENICIA BRIDGE

Pittsburg

RICHMOND BRIDGE

ANGEL I.

ALCATRAZ I.

Oakland

GOLDEN GATE BRIDGE

San
Francisco

S A N   F R A N C I S C O   B A Y

*P A C I F I C

O C E A N*

0   10 MILES